BEARMEN DESCEND UPON GIMLI

BEARMEN DESCEND UPON GIMLI

D.A. Lockhart

fhp Frontenac House Poetry

Series editor: Micheline Maylor
Book design: Neil Petrunia
Cover image: Alberta Rose W./Ingniq
Author photo: D.A. Lockhart

Library and Archives Canada Cataloguing in Publication

Title: Bearmen descend upon Gimli / D.A. Lockhart.
Names: Lockhart, D. A., 1976- author.
Description: Poems.
Identifiers: Canadiana (print) 20210293721 | Canadiana (ebook) 2021029373X | ISBN 9781989466261
(softcover) | ISBN 9781989466308 (PDF)
Classification: LCC PS8623.O295 B43 2021 | DDC C811/.6—dc23

Frontenac House gratefully acknowledges the support of the Canada Council for the Arts for our publishing program. We would also like to thank the Government of Alberta Multimedia Development Fund for their support of our publishing program.

Canada Council for the Arts   Conseil des Arts du Canada   Alberta Government

Printed and bound in Canada
Published by Frontenac House Ltd.
37 Westridge Crescent
Okotoks, AB T1S 0G7
Tel: 403-263-7025

frontenachouse.com

Contents

Marten and Bear Cast Stones: An Origin

Let us sing with open hearts through every
of the twelve heavens to wake Creator,
remind them of how we must move

here upon the turtle's shell, between birch
and pine forests. How each of our relations
has danced in the ways Creation calls us to.

Let this song commence in the shift, release, pull
as we move upon the earth herself, each
move a celebration of struggle, survival.

During grandmother's early revolutions,
Marten greeted days birthed to Creation,
held watch over the still cold earth.

Ice from horizon to horizon, movements atop
measured in ends, looping back, then
forward. Marten flickers about, atop ice

performing a blanket dance to end all seasons,
as if hoping to receive gas money enough
to cross the Great White Way themselves.

He would saunter until Bear awoke, far away north,
and the land and the game and the song
would be rich like the bejeweled sky itself.

Until the day was greeted by Mastodons' arrival,
petulant, hungry in the manner that knows
no end, obdurate as ice incapable of thaw.

Four of them, arrived from the west on ribbon
highways of hot breath into crisp crystalline
air. Each breath an act of rage against Creation.

Their trumpeting, footfall chased Marten from the ice
him and Bear had danced smooth. Visitors
claiming that which is not rightfully theirs,

even the sky and air through their violent lashings.
They built nests upon everything, ate everything,
made horrible songs chasing away all the birds

and game. And Marten grew more hungry, more lonely,
more miserable than he had ever felt. He was
an exile in his own land. Sorrow overcame him

and Marten sang aloud of his loss, his cries
carried the wounding through every
heaven touched by Crow, and shook

the heavens until their celestial clamour
awoke Bear and his relations. South,
they came to the calls of their dear friend.

And Bear with his clan of three, arrived in song,
meeting the mastodons upon iced over
earth, between rock and sky, stood.

Naabe-makwa declared that the land before them
belonged to no one but Creator.
To be awakened by the cries of Marten

was cause enough to upset the even whiteness
of snow, to battle out who holds dominion
over the gifts of Creator. And so, Bear

threw stones of granite into the house of Mastodon.
His relations followed, and between their
two encampments they cast stones against

each other for nine moonrises, and they were led
to a draw. With gnashing teeth and trumpets
Mastodon and his relations declared themselves

the true victors. With others growing despair in defeat,
Crow arrived, burning branch and medicine songs
long forgotten of how Creator favours song and story

over proclamations of might, baseness of insatiable appetites,
violences great and small that are inflicted on others
for one's individual gain. And the fire warmed

their pocket of Creation and the heat brought in more
animals from the east, from the north, and
south. Noozhe-mkwa sang them in. They danced

and sang louder and louder until their chorus drowned
out the trumpets and stomping of the Mastodons.
And the rage of the invaders spiraled into full body

flails and ice shattering foot work. Seeing the cracks beneath
their feet, Marten told Bear and all the animals to cast
their stones into the house of Mastodon. Granite

upon granite they pushed and guided the rocks cast onto
the creaking ice beneath the invaders. In their rage
the Mastodons couldn't hear the world crack apart

beneath them. Mastodon fell beyond the measured shell
of earth, with the world returned to them, Marten,
Bear, and all clans danced beneath the ancestors.

Artificer of Ice

Know that all things commence
in layers laid down as if a lineage
of sediments over epochs, glacial
in the sense that time passes only
as it will not as one believes it must.

Season after season returns, departures
become muscle twitch, arrivals
the necessity of being and each layer
a testament to the way we react
to the world we are given. Follow
as he outlines the means to execute
an end, facilitate the gentle sweep
of broom over ice, the granite cascade
as rock carries a touch's momentum,
outstretched hand dangled in mid-slide.

Time is marked by layers we move upon
and by those we must leave behind. Bits
of slow fought work must reach through
to both proper ends. In Marten spirit,
dancing cold foot forward, side glances,
this one man mists another layer into
being, softly leaves ice beads indiscernible
to those that will play out resultant ends
on the sheet cast in lineage partially his own.

AWAKENING

Rise of the New Prophet

Coax forth the pathway of the ancestors. Let descend their stories upon the head of the Marten in sure-fire descent. That they shall arrive upon waves of warmth cast off by the flaking walls of a double-wide trailer wood stove. Washed over us. Wave followed by wave as if Lake Winnipeg arisen from the restless banks, delivered a summer it has never found. Old men sing the fire of Creation back into the callous Cracking Tree Moon. In these songs, in this rising warmth, feel Creation fall back upon itself, washes out that which was once forgotten.

Upon the Bay
of Shining Waters
draped in
fallen
breath
of Grandfather of the West,
that rocks shall collide
and shake back
at the wounds left
by small men with big guns
and hunger for what is not theirs.

Three months into a world without Dudley George and the lounge between games is aglow like a Tragically Hip album, charged with a darkness that could find form in a well worn sheet with well-placed stones. Believe that the Bearmen awoke when *Grace, Too* bore out and through the lounge jukebox. The slow awakening comes in buckling with will and determination and ends in a harmonic waffle between the lines all people must walk. The Northwind rink had drawn the Police Union rink and the match white board alone told the way that every opening to every medicine album comes with something sweet, something driving, something sure to find its footing in rage.

How sniper rifles rattle
holes through a school bus
and the one shot too many
that pulls breath from Creation.

At the bar, three mustached men hold tightly to their bottles of lakefront beer, brag that the album is one that they played when they busted the grow-op other side of Wasaga. Bartender keeps her distance between them and ice bucket and bar taps. Hairless one returns to the empty seat, proclaims that the only thing between them and the trophy are the "chugs" from the island, that the world knows they might gripe but in the end they all fall like a George in a parking lot with a few well-placed quick slights of hand.

Overheard,
Meldrum Bay rink
    recoils into the bay
waiting
in the quiet
where Indians believe
safety rests.
    strength builds.

Northwind carries some breath back, whispers Dudley into the icebox air two feet above the sheet. The hammer cold against his naked hand and the fluorescent lights hum down their drone of a song that lets him know the ancestors are watching, they too have arrived. Two Heads and Snake posed with brooms just ahead, await the spring and the release. Aimed at the four staggered blue rocks in the house against their red three, the song sings down to Northwind coaxes his movements into the lines and pathways he can't see. This rock must cast out the ones that have come to before them to the sheet. Northwind releases

Cold between the fabric
    of his knees rock unhooks,
spins like sun rising
    to meet moon, hesitates.

And the rock spins down sheet, Northwind hollering to the sweepers, howling medicine songs to guide the broom and slant the world for just a few moments for all of Indian-kind. Snake and Two Heads run clear and free as if a herd of caribou over the ancient open air ridges beneath Lake Huron. Before they hit the first hash mark they peel off to the side. And the sheet is draped in ear ringing quiet.

The peaks and valleys
of water stopped in mid stride
turns rock in cascade,
        curves the path like comet
        streaking an Indiana sky.

Heavy, heaving rupture as granite collides with granite and Northwind regains his feet. Witness as the union stones are cast out of the house. Three red defiant rocks holding the sheet and existence itself in place. Witness the stoic defiance of each rock as Creator delivers the only sort of justice a contemporary treaty Indian could hope for. Proclamations of burnt stones emerge from the opposition.

Two Heads runs first
        as if a moose is winged
        and must be caught before
        it escapes. Mid-stride
he grabs the Esso Foley Township
Bonspiel Trophy.
        Bursts out rink doors
        before complaints ensue.

Northwind delivers the blow that dislodges him from Ontario curling. Delivers it with the same broom that he bent Creation with. And the cheers and protestations collapse back to the hum of fluorescent lights as the Union skip face plants into empty cups and used towels. Through the lounge each gaping stride of the only way to win battles out of your territory. Northwind runs through the rink, out of the lounge, every step leveraged

In the path of Snake
into Two Heads'
grand caravan
Eagles' *Already Gone*
delivering honour beats
into the night,
victorious
Meldrum Bay rink burning
up bridges all the way
back to the rock of Manitoulin.

Northwind Receives Council from Tommy Myers at Gore Bay, Esso Station

Gossip crossed the bridge,
          auntie fast, mere hours after
Two Heads' Grand Caravan.

"Those that would challenge
          cops, looked to bring trouble."

And the elders spoke
          at the VFW ,
          over lunch specials,
reminded all that could hear
since Tecumseh fell at Fairfield,
winning meant running.

Northwind had won his trophy.

Myers rings up pepperettes
          mentions lunch with others
          offers good council
given to the ancestors
when Waawiiyaatanong
became Detroit; flight.

Ipperwash was about walking
where we weren't supposed to;
          Golf courses, pocket electronics,
          curling trophies, are keys
          to the Great White Way.

Snap of leathery skin
          between
          molars.
          Spice,   heat,   floods in.

One shouldn't need a sweat
to witness how the Next Fire
bursts forth
　　　　from a bonspiel trophy.

After *Just For Laughs,*
　　　　Myers hibernated for three commercial breaks
　　　　had the simple vision:

Take what is yours
Find the warriors.
They arrive in dreams and visions.
　　　　When we are ready.
　　　　When Creation is ready.
　　　　Northwind is a new prophet.

Northwind Births Waabizheshi-Anangoog at the Waters of Meldrum Bay

A trinity of chrome
plastic columns
should rise above
faux marble platform
uphold the coiled
blue, red, white
of corporate petroleum
clans, this declaration

of what dutifully shall be gifted
from John A. MacDonald, Indian
land distilled to the celebration
of two hundred years of treaties
and the medicine widgets off-duty
cops can fight for between Labatt 50
drafts. The trophy glistens
with a thousand horrible medicines.

Remove the head and the beast shall die.

Northwind clear cuts
the trophy top, hums
Glen Campbell, pulverizes
plastic with Meldrum Bay
beach rocks. Decades old
glue hold fast glitter
of crushed plastic
onto a skull,
deposited by the lake
beyond.

His hands guided by his song,
move without thought,
and form the long slope
of a pine marten,
encrusted in the light
of at least three generations.

Tecumseh and Girty Deliver Vision of the Great Black Snake

It floats in, as if it were a fog bank
arriving from the lake, seeking safety.
Dissipates to island VFW interior, flush
with Charlie Pride Choctaw medicine
strung before Northwind like crystal
chandeliers. Northwind pours to darkened
regions of tavern, moving with fog
as it peters into even light and shadow,
to the booth between trophy case
and emergency exit. Pineapple-glass
table-top candle makes majestic
refractions across council faces.

Girty translates laminated menu;
          white bread, Klik luncheon slab,
          yellow mustard garnish. Ruffles sides,
          Delmonte fruit and syrup cups. Admits
to Tecumseh herein lies the gifts afforded
by the Battle of the Thames, friendships
with British generals. He offers Northwind
a handful of Corn Nuts. They crunch like
granite, unleash ranch coolness to tongue.

Nearby, a television replays Ron Maclean
commentary on the Briar Cup Tragedy
as if oil had been discovered untouched below
every Upper Canadian small town curling club.
A buffoon in a multicoloured suit hollers
about old-time curling, and that real
men live off Alberta crude, punch others
when at all possible. Girty explains the man's
fire is waning. Erection drugs get more air time.

Tecumseh leans in, explains:
          learn the ice. The Marten will return
          and with the Bear cousins shall wound
          the Snake that blocks our path forward.

Northwind Hears Her Voice First at Wawa

He awakens beneath
            the giant goose.
            Trophy tucked
            into duffle bag,
            Pendleton blanket
            wrapped, and him
            atop concrete sidewalk.
            Outstretched wings

cold, lifeless. This is no place
to be holed up for more than
a night. And so, he moves.

Through the wind, a song
ancient like motion
                        between
            trees and rock and snow,
                        breaks

alongside an
            empty   highway.

Sundown on the TransCanada

Sometimes I think it's a sin when I feel like
I'm winning when I'm losing again.
You can picture every move that a man can make,
yet, sometimes I think it's a sin when I feel like
running to the places that your past is cold smoke
in the wind. Move, move nijii, later you win.
Sometimes I think it's a sin when I feel like
I am winning when I'm losing again. Moving again.

This Fire Born of Distant Volcanoes

Glaciers, fire, molten rocks seven time
zones distant, brought a Norse village
through a continent's freshwater heart.
Heat in the aggression of coal cooked
steam, pushed them inland to a one-mile
frontage of the great Cree inland sea.

Those in flight took refuge against sea,
shaken land, in Gimli they began time
anew. Pyroclastic lightning scored one-mile
of home into the footprints of a sometimes village
bisected by Hudson Bay trade routes, cooked
in prairie's edge summer sun, cold heart

Manitoba winters consort, here is the heart
of a continent. Here, too, along muddy sea,
Northwind sets down his exile. Life cooked
down into a double-wide lodge, bought in time
sold to janitorial services. Outside the village
of Norse men, and view of sky and lake one-mile

wide if not more, Northwind basks on his one-mile
of exile, Waabizheshi-Anangoog Trophy the heart
of his double wide, atop a wood box tv, his village
within four walls, and at properties edge sea
of Lake Winnipeg, his wood stove measures time
in consumption of wood chords, land cooked

into quiet comfort, reminiscent of calm cooked
up by a warrior accustomed to victory, any village
is the stop between battles, he understands time
is that which makes familiar an exile, whose heart
knows at best war is survival. Meldrum Bay was a sea
of shield and grass and roads away, his village

still haunted by shadow play of OPP snipers, village
surrounded by mythologies earned in tragedy, cooked
to molten stew by wretched colonial sins, sea
that protection medicine he required. Each mile
an added sprinkle of bagijigan, proof of a heart
given unwillingly to exile. He rests here for a time.

Towards the village, from his one-mile of shore,
he sends cooked wood smoke into heart of sky,
that limitless sea, believes time has circled round.

Waabizheshiwayaan

TransCanada marten
fur sways in wind, gestures
westward in dance.

Eddie Puskamoose Showers History at the Main Street ACE Hardware

At its heart the Bear
Clan protects us,
Puskamoose declares.
Our peoples need
aggression that modern
Canada makes us smile
at being inappropriate.

Drops deck screws,
clearance twine, two
packs of Thrills
atop counter. Bears,
cousins to spirits,
Creator lets loose
to haunt our north.

He says he's seen them,
waking up in the static
of his TV when Global
goes off air for night,
bothered by post anthem
white noise, he knows
they've come in season.

In keeping with ancient
teachings, town Cree
like him don't follow.
He first saw them after
a Scott Tournament
of Hearts replay. Heard
hunger in their stirrings.

Persistent Clatter of Dreams

They arrive first in adamantine
dreams of reflective ice sheets
the hollers of men as they move
rock with a twist of wrist, end
in vignettes of what the spirit
knows the body must do. Time
measured in the things that one
doesn't do, the waking between,
selling hardware at local ACE.

Haunted by tectonic thud of
season-end bird baths, Northwind
caught in refusal to sleep, sits
on the top fresh cedar step
of his double-wide. Witnesses
the storm approaching from
the lake. Winter will know
wind, Gimli will shake, distant
grunts of trees speak to a rise
of Bears, their winter sleep
something that will wait until.

After the Last Streetlight Fires in Gimli

At a point, Northwind stops desiring rest
as rest returns glimpses
of bed medicine
artifacts, echoes
the twelve heavens above.

Above, heavens revolve around
the Gimli Recreation Centre
the wheel spins
and the ancestors turn
blurring Creation
to red white yellow black

Northwind, perched in lounge
watches CTV News on the only
tv working and the bartender
keeps vigil over her cell phone
and Northwind's cranberry juice.
Three fingers on the rocks.

The last lights of Gimli fire
into this nascent night
and he knows he must leave.
His sense that the next vision
he will not awake from.
And it shall carry him forth
the twelve heavens above revolve
and it shall carry him forth.

Prophet Returns, Tells of Nations Gathering

Night cut open by a meteor,
torn from west to south,
colonisation as if a panther
had gouged the darkness
between ancestors, Northwind
in cut-offs, April Wine shirt,
the transistor crackle of *Sundown,*
Lightfoot heavy on the tempest,
in ambulant darkness, musket
Sea-Doo drone heralds the arrival
of flip-flop Tecumseh, his attorney
Simon Girty. April Wine pours
into deep tracks and Northwind
tastes Molson Stock Ale as if
it were cottonwood pollen
in a Muskoka late spring.

In absence of earthquakes
and redcoats, Tecumseh speaks
of nations rather than
confederacies, how being dead
at the right time makes you
the spokesperson for the wrong
people, and the gathering is the end
of all that is right. Girty delivers
a gift of granite rock, well formed
from beyond the shoreline.
Tecumseh, rock in hand
measures the evenness of water,
before skipping its impossible
weight across the wave tops
and falls into a house a good
fifty-seven feet out.

Girty proclaims granite
is the anchor between worlds,
every point along the white path
knows the pull of granite
as it rests within its house.

They slip out by the first cracks
of daylight, Northwind awakens
to CBC Winnipeg and weather for
Gimli-Lake Winnipeg and region.

Northwind Returns to Curling through the Preparation of Beef and Greens

Begin in iron cast black as lake bottom
fat rendered to coat its surface in an oil
slick most modern Indians come to fear
or fight or worse. But this timeless way
to render sweetness from bitter plant,
this gift that glistens as it receives browned
flesh, awaits the tenderness of cooked leaves,
warms the air, sweetens the room around it.

Return to the clap of broom ends and cheek
bone, return to the ecstatic glide atop ice,
swirl the flesh in the bath of agitated oil
and heat, feel that every motion of arm,
every passion of anger leads a man here,
to gifts being doled out, roles to be honoured
with. Together, heat, oil, flesh, and greens
are the love that no woman, no trophy gives.
Northwind faces west, soon to eat alone
at a Giant Tiger card table to CBC Radio.

The love part, he is sure perched beneath
the peat of the Orkey Islands, reserved
for men with fine whisky last names,
but passions can be unqualified affairs
and the places where history and curling
meet extend outward from there. As if
glaciers have returned with mastodons, low
seas, and free movement, he awaits cooked
romance, dreams of the way history
returns with a single plea into a winter sky.

Vinyl Benches

Northwind considers visions
of lake bottom granite
of pan-seared greens
of wounds that grow
from an absence fluent
to exiles.

Saccharine mixed-blood coffee
muffles the crueller
sweetness, donut shop
afternoon exudes how
nations meet on treaty
land.

Receiver of visions he knows
are incomplete.
That Martens dance
awaiting their kin,
and life has unfinished
business

that follows one across time, across many lives.

Dream of the Spacemen Arriving

In the lustre of a morning
slept through the mind
searches for every majestic
way to enter Gimli, over
a wind-stirred lake bow cutting
into the soapstone of water,
gravel dust petering out two
kilometers above outstretched
pine, know that arrival comes
by way of the Tim Horton's
drive thru, only one passed
off in the bag of taste-free
sandwiches, this vision
comes in familiar as if family
arriving, the ones well-fed
but empty-handed, put up
on the advancing side
of town, in accommodations
streamlined for Trans-Canada
stop-overs, faux wood
and rose-leaf furniture
that says what lies around
us, is collateral for that
which must do.

Northwind Receives the Western Canada Lottery Corporation Vision

Outward from the bedrock concrete
of Portage and Main, the announcement
arrives like an opened-wing hawk, settling
in behind a retreating Red River, rattling
forth in speaker sound from Northwest
Thrift Store TVs. Between Blue Bombers
downs and ways one burns away
in late season CFL games, emerges every
other thing one should have done. Two
decades later, now in Gimli, accept that
one learns to listen for medicine songs
in the rattles and shakes of metal.
Grasp that trailer walls vibrate songs
and dances and stories that have passed
before Northwind. Many enough to think
about years later. Belief leads one to
epiphany, understand Creator determines
that time. Northwind does, follows
the vision of a smooth, well-marked
sheet. Beaded in the way that grass
becomes ice along lake edge. Northwind
feels the ice as his child, him the artificer
of a clean sheet of perfection atop frozen
earth. Line playing through his head
like petroglyphs along a Lake Huron
shore, Bring A Bonspiel Home,
suburb choir cheerfulness in each note.
Apply today. Be the man you must be.

When he comes to, still on his feet
he stands before the glassware shelves
sight rested on wood tipped tumblers,
each emblazoned with a large stoic bear.

Northwind purchases the set of bear
tumblers, leaves into high cold autumn
sun of a cloudless sheet flat lake town.

Dream of the Marten Along the Shore

Between the iridescent light
snowfall and wide-open blue
of a January northern sky, he is
soapstone black, a carving misplaced
in the threshold between sand
and ice. He stands, chin against
westerlies, each gust a moment
that snaps against the lake mirage
behind him, light swaying like grass
dancers on day three of Norway House
Pow-wow. Northwind knows him
from that look, determined to keep
at bay things which may emerge
from behind the homes, beyond
the flood plain trees and disrupt
the manner that light falls, rises,
and whirls above the lake frozen
months ago, in mid-caress of land
he may never know in any way.

Sven Pedersen Receives Sauna Vision from Northwind

In truth, men of the land
received omens, visions,
dreams in the ways rocks
beneath us come to tell us.

Northwind rests in late morning darkness. Import of a healing lodge from distant volcanic islands, at ease in the non-hereditary chief's two-storey snout house well into the forest line skirting Gimli. All nations finding their foothold in the land rested upon, discover Creation's voice, understand its needs in the subterranean darkness and heat. Sven Pedersen holds this two-man, late morning council, in the sauna at the rear of the two-car garage with a house built around it.

Heat in steam from the drip line
of a chieftain's hand, pine adorned
room draws sweat from within
pulls powers from deepest roots.

Seven generations up these Cree shores. And words tumble out like silt from a northern island, truthful, honest, slow layering of a foothold in ever-shifting land. Northwind comes to speak of martens along the shore, Bearmen tumblers, and thrift shop visions. The words that will deliver Bearmen, spacemen, and miners to town. Permissions to be sought from the holders of the land he makes camp upon.

No question. Snow comes
when it must. Hibernation
ends when it must. These
are the way with all things.

Waters scour scant cold from the room. Glow of rocks the dim light, everlasting glow of this council fire. Pedersen agrees that omens and dreams must be heeded. Gimli must be roused from hibernation, must prepare and embrace the gifts given to it.

Crow Carries the Word to the Three Oceans

So word arrives
          jagged and rich like the flame burnt
          caw of crow through mid-winter snow
          reminding Creation of sacrifices
          and the certainty one just fights to survive,
          that most losses are pride and pride
          is what often negates how one survives.

It ripples through CBC weekend
daytime ad blocks,
          cut screens
          on the CHL game of the week,
the weekly circulars of small northern towns.

Crow arrives
          in television
          wave ether
          with word.

Black ragged in utilitarian bird song:
          Gimli Trans National Bonspiel
          Cracking Tree Moon
          $50,000 Grand Prize
          daily 50/50
          (518)876-7412
          ask for Gretta.

Gretta Van Winston is Comforted by a Vision of Bearmen

Impatient twitch of call arriving
to her desk phone, red light
siren into a long morning
that wears on Gretta. Another
fire greeted with indifference.

Buzz arriving email
sprouts video of Noozhe-mkwa,
"We have heard. Bear Cousins
have awoken. We shall arrive."
And she hums a stove-warmed
condensed milk song as it ends.

Gretta knows comfort
in the songs of the she-bear,
recalls their melodies and
is wrapped in spine tingle
warmth of their strength.

Witnesses the finesse
of middle bear, a balance
of 20 pack of Timbits upon
a single braid of sweet grass.
Sweetness upon medicine.

Feels the grumble of power
from the largest bear,
able to change the tire
of a conversion van
without a proper jack.

And in their presence,
the blinking red light
falls silent, and Gretta
bathes in paper cut
movements below air duct.

Northwind Dreams She Makes Fire Dance

From hibernation
Noozhe-mkwa
arises first.

Northwind witnesses
her rouse from pleather
sofa,
the first chimes
of Floyd's *Wish*
You Were Here

And her stretching
becomes fire
above a snow-
locked town.

She stirs to motion
upon the sweetness
of crow's words

Motion becomes fire.

Fire dances
as if ancestors
coaxing Creation
back upon the path
it must take.

Fire mirrored
from inside earth
ignites within
Northwind.

Northwind Returns Home Past Midnight

Fresh snow across deck
leading from shadows to lake
reveals bear print pathway.

RISEN

The Arrival

In the world that would see Pelletier
and Means as sentinels to that line
that cuts treaty land from prison,
their names would be shouted out,
across ice that transforms this lake
into a highway, booming outward
like the grand entrance call bringing
in dancers straight off Rocky Boy plains,
Northwind can hear them descending.

Throughout this poorly insulated night,
drafty like an Indian Affairs' trailer,
they arrive in the red-glow night light
cast by a GMC Conversion the colour
of last spring's run-off and Redbone doing
their best to coax Gale Whitefeather back
to the campground with each easy croon.

It is all come and get your love and the quiet
of warriors before putting down camp. Arrival,
in this world cast after sunset, they pull
up before Northwind's place and unload
every last man and their gear before any
treaty agents could make note of the newest
conversion van to hold-up outside Northwind's
lakeside single-wide on the outskirts of town.

Night returns to the hustle of clouds ushered
across open spaces of stars against the deep
blue of groaning ice and distant restless trees.

Bearmen Greet Fresh Day, Hibernation Ends

Greet this dim morning
through the rise of steam
from hand-me-down CBC
mugs, the crackling of ham
heated against Teflon. Laugh
at how poorly Dudley rolls
cigarettes nearly three decades
in and the thickness of frost on
single pane windows understand
this ceremony is accompanied
by creaking floor soft spots
and the thud of ceramic against
vinyl tabletops. Nosemaskwa sleeps
the men await dawn to pass,
Creation to burn to life, their sister
to awaken and sing the rink alive
into this gathering at the edges
of Cree land and the waters beyond.

Lacroix Arrives at New Iceland

Functional in every way,
the box-top hotel stares
onto the street with a shadow
that cuts lake edge lines deeper

Through sun-dappled snow-pile streets
linger half sprouts of a summer
lake town that holds a gateway
to the north of controlled movement

From his hotel room, he makes out
mostly naked trees, rotation
of earth beneath clouds, absence
of any ground-level movement
yet the sun leaves and returns
passing in waves.

Lacroix notes the hard edges
of Gimli, prods for soft spots,
knows he must understand
this earth as his, see that one
Bonspiel win is worth three
Canadarm satellite recoveries.

TWO STOREYS UP

the world is less lines and hash marks
more the way Creation contorts itself to us.

Nickelmen Set Camp in Outskirts of Gimli

Flin Flon the crooked line
between here and nowhere
the five men arrive through
a tangle of lakes and rivers
and rock to Fred Jorgenson's
place on highway 154.

Expedition pock-marked
like roadside granite outcrops
            greetings as the procession
            ends at driveway, they arrive.

They shall exist in the dim light
            beyond the last shadows
            of town. Inside those
lines the places angry wives
            and handsome paychecks deposit
            them. But this, this is work
            and the way fortunes changed.

From Sobeys Emerges the Short Order Rink

Ice, salt, gun metal slurry
aglow in box store
light cavalcade.

They emerge single file
smoke skyward, deer
crossing empty highways.

That they emerge far too long after sunset
is innate like the hunger for better, for belonging.

Returned to the overstuffed
minivan, four men speak
of meat cuts, seasoning,

the weight of curling
stones against tired arms,
emptiness of bank accounts.

Unpaid leave taken in a town built
from the spite of working men dreams.

Grand Caravan pulls off,
glides to outskirts motel
where rusted rocker panels

shall be brushed smooth
and glistening like ice
before rock, after footfall

and in dreams to follow, the belief stews that through
sheer will they shall come to be known as curlers.

Roughneck Rink Arrives from Treaty Eight Land

Night itself, aglow.
Oxide crimsons, liquid
oranges, sulfide yellows,
distant oil patches paint
the sky after their hunger.

All of the world burns
from distant fires.
Blue and white
of motel capture
the light, draw it in.

Their arrival marked
in the seven-truck convoy,
single occupant exhaust cast
between
swaying truck nuts,
nose-to-tail,
they arrive

with vision only of themselves.
Men willing to fracture
the Earth itself
to feed their insatiable hunger.

Nineteen-ton pack mules
shake the earth beneath them
as if they alone lay claim, as if they
shall rip right through past lake
bottom and dig up all that is theirs.

AUTUMN WOOD
MOTEL

Sways atop shifting earth.
Whispers *vacancy* beneath.

Equilibrium of Body, Firmness of Nerve

Northwind explains into headlight
exposed lake surface the motion
of martens, cooperation of quickness,
nerve, deceptive might. Nosemaskwa
whirls a six-pace round dance, drags
cascading footfalls through chaos,
memory, control. Motion is control.

Step atop wind-blown
ice, hours identified
in toe ground snow
she steps, slides along.

Bear and Marten are cousins, strike
at those that hinder how Creation
must be. Believe that men who live
cutting holes through rock, do not
fear the strength of the Bear.

Her steps across

ice

vanish outside

the light.

Wind pours

from west,

moved by

ancestor breaths

Mistahaya turns to the shore
line, pisses against rocks, returns
with a Rothman's medicine stick.
Follows Northwind through clan
dance intertribal with equilibrium
of a small man, the granite nerve
of creature all too willing to kill.

Grandfather of the West Meets Grandmother of the South above Gimli

The settlers called it an Alberta Clipper
Northwind knew from Old Frank Waabooz
that when the coyotes forgot their medicine
songs the grandparents would get all
sort of frisky above you, cracking tree
moons the worst time of all. Sitting
in the vinyl deck chairs he had left
out too long three years ago, Northwind
shares a joint with Nosemskwa across
a treated wood valley in the building
through-wind, and is awed by the quiet
of the night. Feels Waabooz's tales in the
crooks of knees and tells Nosemskwa
to get medicine, there is a storm coming.
Her voice familiar like wind, pine, AM
radio, and Lightfoot on the highway west.

Nosemaskwa Sings Buffy Sainte-Marie to Greet Winter Storm

Misters, can't you see the wind a blowing,
snow a heaving across this frozen lake?
Inside this trailer, winter ain't for sleeping
Misters, can't you see the wind a blowing?
Creator's a stirring, pine trees are a bending
This time our rink this bonspiel will take.
Misters, can't you see the wind a blowing,
snow a heaving across another frozen lake?

Nickelmen Call Their Gods to No Avail

Grandfather of the West,
Grandmother of the South,
            stir Creation into the frenzy
of a world turned against its order.

Nickelmen, far from home,
shelter against the tempest,
            they sing out against
            the wind, the stirrings
            of timeless relations.

Old pallet wood, scraps
of food wrappers, ancient
            magazines and fliers, tossed
onto the pyre. To cast light
from goods paid for with
money earned pulling
chunks from the earth.

Snow fell harder,
blotting out more
of their fire
            with
            billows
            of
            snow
            descending
            from James Bay
            itself.

None of their relations answer
in this place that is not theirs.

Through wind-swept veils
of snow, sets of eyes,
hundreds
watching
pouring back
the artificial
light cast at
them.

Ceremony of the Shaking Double Wide

Accelerated wind
bows and bends walls
trailer thin. Three bears
sleep through worst
of it.

Nosemaskwa,
Northwind,
staggered on couch.
Scent of freshly ignited
campfires on her hair,

the tipsy air
before the storm.
He feels drunk
like he's with
cousins at Gore Bay.

North of 60 plays,
TeeVee chasing
French Canadian rapists
to Lynx River's airport.
Winning is losing.

Concentration
not on process,
but gentle warmth
of her scent, softness
he has not felt

since '06 xmas,
a tussle with Gretta
because her nerves
and it's the fibre
of small towns.

Northwind knows
this is how it begins
to end, because vision
has it when things
work, this is the path.

Ceremony commences
as credits roll.
Fictional RCMP
saving Native youth
from Stoney Mountain.

Unrequited revenge,
left to simmer, enough
to scare the worst settlers
into coexistence.
Winning is losing.

This is justice in
a treaty-denying
world. And she
follows in ceremony
folding her body

against his.
Ceremony unfolds
like an old time story
of ghosts from a wishing
well. The walls of the double wide

shakes back
at the world, from the inside
and shook the heavens until
their celestial clamour awoke
his relations.

Chocolate Walnut Cruller Vision

Begin with winter sunlight
made heavy and warm with
passage through plate glass
store front. Find Northwind
in line between donut counter
and first rows of tables.

An exchange results in cedar
tea and a chocolate walnut
cruller being placed before
Northwind. Girty explains
contained in that sugar plated
chocolate dough is all the good
the British Empire left us.

Tecumseh laughs with Girty,
recalls a bakeshop at Detroit,
a fine view of the Savoyard,
admits to missing the settler
city like one misses the causes
of hangovers. He reminds
Northwind to save some
donuts for the woman beside
him. And the two sing in unison

> *what's the matter with you*
> *feel right, don't you feel right?*
> *Hey, oh yeah, get it from*
> *the divine, cause its fine. All*
> *too fine. Go and get more love.*

And the light is warmer
than sunlight on Gore Bay,
than the dry heave of air
from his woodstove, than
the cold air outside the sheets.

Upon the Horizon

Lacroix, eyes fixed to horizon
          awaits
          the ascent   and   transit
          of the ISS through
                    the bands
                              of gathering clouds.

An ember
then spark
and radiant glow
on the horizon.

He senses danger,
          that fire
under circumstances,
related not entirely to
atmospheric conditions,
indicate mechanisms outside
of one's rational control.

And his world, from here
          and above
                    is
                    rational
                    control.

Distant flames,
          whipped into rolling
          rhythm, then writhing
          in ribbons of snow.
Red like Mars itself
and this astronaut
wise enough to know
          himself a witness
          to an omen,

that finds footing with
distant synapses telling
Lacroix, on this night
    that path of events
    had been determined
    by the dance
    of Marten
    in the sky
    above
    this
    Manitoba
    town.

MAAJISE

Bonspiel Begins.

"When winter muffles up his cloak,
And binds the mire like a rock,
Then to the loch the Curlers flock
Wi' gleesome speed."
~ Robert Burns

God's Lake Dawn Awakes Gimli for the First Day of Bonspiel

"It was the custom in Paisley, not many years ago, to send the town drummer, after two- or three-nights' hard frost, to proclaim to the inhabitants where the curlers should meet in the morning."
~ Jacks Bicket, *the Canadian Curler's Manual.*

Day awakens with the bugle
of Jordan Leduc from the flatbed
of Northwind's '89 Dodge, rolling
through the side streets of town
like sparrows between town hedges,
Swampy Cree cousins pulling up reeds
of nighttime, peeling back sleep
of settlers and Vikings alike.
Mistahaya in thunderbird regalia
leading the path to Peter Glint
Memorial Curling Rink, fanning
outward spin of feathers and ribbon
and colour through the snow
and indigo of first light. Each
ramped up call by Leduc, every
feather blend of snow, risen
to Creation above, declaring
Treaty I land is leased land
and the landlords have returned
to move stone, carve their ways
again into ice and stories to come.

Sixteen Stones in Staggered Motions

With each end measured
in sixteen individual
releases,
through eight distinct
points
of friction

10 ends,
73 minutes,

the civilized means
measured rounds
of conflict. Staggered
in turns. Redcoats
in regimental lines
ripe for harvest
ripe for killing
ripe for honouring
the warriors
who knew better
than to leave
the tree line.

7 rinks
5 days

certainty afforded by vision
the willingness to dance
through process, to feel
loss and know that fires
will follow. Know that vision
has foretold the future.
We must now simply
dance ourselves to the end.

Mistahaya Stalks Val D'Or at Morning Practice

Inland, between backs of pine and
aluminum wrapped community rink
they gather in quiet. Northwind
watching the mining men throw stones.
Bearmen reclined, propped up
against vinyl booth backs. Patterns
on the sheets behind lounge windows
mirror moose migrations in dusk
spirit moonlight. The glaze cast off
between double-doubles and apple
fritters is a sweet post-dawn gossamer.
Through it, Mistaya stares down
their movements with hunger, each
rip, each curl, each slide of broom.
They retreat when the Val d'Or
men take heed of Mistahaya gaze.,
having sensed the storm has moved
in from across the lake.

Northwind Places Waabizheshi-Anangoog atop the Lounge Fireplace at the Peter Glint Memorial Curling Rink

Withdrawn from
    My Compliments grocery bag
    Northwind retrieves the angular
    trophy, unshields Waabizheshi-
    Anangoog from the world.

And it discovers
    a new resting space. Above
    lounge fireplace, warmed
    from below, patchwork body
    catches and reflects light

from above.
    Returns it to the room,
    familiar, with warmth,
    yet changed through acts
    of history, reflective yet new.

Nosemaska Sacrifices Bagpipes to Protection Medicine

She witnesses it arrive
            in car 6340,
            RCMP guarded,
and from that, understands
            its essence to be evil.

That they wail into air
akin to a lynx in heat,
            there is a certain
            terror, a wound
            up aggression within
            pipes of Gimli.

Their cry not akin to drum
connecting relations
            to the stone
            to the sky
            to the gifts
            of Creation.

Wailing is the song
of people drowning
            out others,
            of history
            over present,
            of place not here.

She heard the wails
from the yard behind
the Curling Club. Spots
the creature   and
            its keepers emerge
from the hollow shell
of an RCMP wagon.

She explains to Officer Holm,
that Timbits
and coffee are free
to service men inside.

She lies in wait,
in the smoker's pit,
as the officers
enter rink. Across
empty lot, she
walks to car

retrieves blue green
tartan skin bag
from back seat,
carries them, their
dark medicine songs,
of death, of darkness

imported from land
clear cut by colonisers,
raped for centuries,
and deposited here,
she cradles the bag,
drones, reeds

hanging loose like
an animal clinging
to life, carries it
to pine tree stand
behind the rink
and tosses them

into the thicket high
above
her outstretched
arms.

Northwind Exchanges Niceties with the Nickel Men

Hotplate reconstituted eggs glow
marigold neon, establishing themselves
in the distant corner of the lounge.
Northwind with a plate of desiccated
sausage links and reanimated, scent-
free eggs, established at the bar.

They spoke first, like relations of rock
were ought to do. Waited upon, they deliver
distant songs of the earth beneath us.
He claimed to hear the rock sing
against the palm of his hand. Trick
was to make them dance down ice.

They asked of the Bearmen. Spoke of how
the mines back home groaned like an old
tired and hungry bear before spring.
Like all rock, it was the silences that
spoke. Each one portioned out terror
that the unspoken could rain true.

To be known as the single fugitive in Canada
curling, means to have power like Indians
before Oka, before Little Big Horn,
all mystics receiving comet visions,
and selling superior cheap tobacco
and rock shavings that pass as arrowheads.

When rock is unsteady, the lightest kick
can topple the world. Through dreams, through
song and vision, Northwind understood
the harmonics of rock. He spoke of their
relations. He spoke of the eggs that jiggled
against his fork. He spoke of bears, migration.

Mistahaya Replaces 1983 Children's Anthem Cassette with Redbone

Panic arrives in lounge,
        as Officer Holm
returns, proclaims Gimli
to be a thieves' den. Sacred
skin bag has been taken.

Sven calms Holm
        with stories
of bears stealing
        lawnmowers, overturning
        parking meters.
Proclaims such crimes
to be the taxes one pays
                to live lakeside
                in a land-locked
                town.

Overheard: THE RECORDING
                of Ms. Laine's class
                anthem version
has always sufficed the situation.

Retrieved from Conversion Van
tape deck,
        Memorix D60, pastel
        triangles, teal squares,
GODS LAKE MIX VOL. 4
upon   peeling   tape.

In the final fade, there arrives
a garbled chorus of nations,
before an abrupt crackle
        and silence
as the final threads
of thin stretched magnetic
tape, snaps through.

Marten chirps this:
get it together, baby.

The Last End of the First Rink

Fur trappers
move frozen rink top
with sweeping brooms.

The physicists watch as the seventh red stone
curls into white stones leaving an empty house.

The last end
and Churchill's stones
will face a Cree hammer.

Mistahaya compliments skip Lacroix
on a rock well placed, as slate worked clean

shared pathways cut
past dwarf trees, muskeg
in nerve-twitch migration

to this regional to pull from the purse of inherited
names; this annual return to conflicts still past.

Let it curl.
red top handle whirls
the rock finds home

sits crow-like atop a fifteen-foot-wide remembrance
of Gods Lake before the space port at Churchill.

Dudley guides
the hammer tossed stone
by dry ended broom.

And two maskwanapewak cloaked in argyle stretch pants
burn a path that chases visitors from their ancestral home.

Short Order Rink Comes to Ice, Falls

Crucifix clutched
in palm of fingerless
glove. Murmured

prayers to a namesake saviour. Blessing from virgin
mother, followed by awkward slide and release.

Stone dervish glides
down ice sheet, brooms,
sweeps unable to keep

ahead. And it spins past the house, over hash
marks, ricochets back at sheet bumpers, rests

beyond scoring.
Roughnecks deliver
ice cutting shots

landing every claim in the dead centre of house,
alone they hold the house end after end. Jesus

speaks beatitudes
to teammates. Offers
encouragement

to unsteady footing on ice, hard grips released
outside of time, the burning of stones by footfall.

Roughneck proclamations
of go back to Mexico,
this is how real Canadians win.

It ends as it begins: prayers to a namesake saviour,
thanks for the chance to learn opportunity lives in bloodlines.

Nosemaskwa Witnesses the Roughneck Violence

Not the loss, nor the humour
          of witnessing others
          being without guides
          in a strange place,
fumbling, flailing, searching
for footholds.

Unanswered prayers
for grace, for thanks,
          and her watching
          from behind lounge
          glass. While

Roughnecks trumpeted
around the house,
          stomped, making
          cacophonous songs
of pre-emptive victories,
of everything given to them
that has come from the violences
of their ancestors, their relations.

And she knows
          that these are distant
          relations, unaware
of the dances, the songs,
the gestures that this portion,
their new portion, of Creation
responds to.

Northwind Holds Council with Jesus

Call to council arises
from cook-out smoke
in cold damp air rising
from parking lot, far side.

Jesus emerges from slide
door of minivan, chorus
of Rodriguez's *Cause,*
aids his descent into cold.

Northwind leads with rolled
Sago offerings, Jesus
reciprocates in rolled
tortilla and chorizo.

And they call down
their relations, with talk
of how they ended up
behind the Peter Glint
Memorial Curling Rink,
calling clans, understanding
the earth beneath them
is a gift that belongs
to no single person,
or group of people.
They stood where
they stood as a gift
from Creation itself.

Distance between old
stock Canada and pre-
Canada measured diameter
between men inside, here
proximity by shared food,
shared embrace of a land
they were born to inhabit.

Nosemaskwa Guides Short Order Rink

"All of Creation
is but a dance,
one foot in contact
with earth, the other
in motion, sweeping
you along the path
you must follow.

Smoothness of ice
as your foot stretched
flat to it, feel the
effortless glide, subtle
touches of ice
refusing to be
even, ice resisting.

This is how you
shall know the challenge,
by touch, by motion,
by how all Creation
holds you up as you
move effortless atop
water gone to hibernate,
that you, yourself are
Creation. That you
shall guide the stone
that too slides atop
ice, and that shall
release it when it asks,
because that is the gift
you are best afforded."

Baptiste crosses himself
thankful for these gifts
laid before him.

Northwind Speaks to Nosemaskwa About the Marten

Together, before the warmth
of *Magnum P.I.* beaches and
last century colour palettes,
          Nosemaskwa
          Northwind
          consume warmth
of wood stove and onscreen
paradise.

Others in slumber.

She speaks of Higgins
          as perfect oppressor,
          occasionally kind,
generally unbending will
the guiding hand that ensures
the right skin tint and bloodline
          make winning possible.

Northwind speaks of Marten
          to Nosemaskwa,
          dreams of dead prophets,
visits in coffee shops, roadside
attractions, the reality
between worlds.

She answers that Marten
          are the closest relations
          to Bears. That they protect
what they can, how best they can
by finesse and kinship.

As Magnum outsmarts
    coloniser attack dogs
    to borrow the Italian
    sports car, she admits
it was the cries of Marten
that awoke her
    and her brothers.
    That she knows
    violence lies ahead.

Nosemaskwa Sings Robbie Robertson to the Ancestors

You don't stand a chance against our prayers.
We shall live again, we shall live again.
Hear this, settlers on shore, we are heirs,
you don't stand a chance, against these prayers.
Each way these rocks cut lines like a surveyor,
above them we shall rise, over Creation reign.
You don't stand a chance, with all these prayers.
We shall live again, we all shall live again.

Ancestors Jingle Dance Above Lake Winnipeg

Between Grandmother
and Fisher, they jingle
their electric green, blue
ribbons across the cloud
free sky. Crackles like tobacco
greeting tongues of fire.

They strut, clear to dawn,
as if a mother bear voice
sang once, churns round
and round the lake shore,
sopping up each moment
of crystalline vapour breath
before daylight saturates it all.

Lacroix Discusses Polar Wanderings with Dudley Over Westerns

Second day begins
with pancakes,
Dudley brooding
over Windspeaker
classifieds, cooling
coffee, warming
orange juice.

Lacroix joins him
at first table in
from fireplace,
Waabizheshi-Anangoog
watches them
with ninety fires
burning back.

They came to agree
upon many things:

We are a species
given to wander,
the sky our guide.
Magnetic fields
that unseen force
pushing, pulling
us from ocean
to ocean to prairie
to mountain top,
is but one true guide.

And so, this rink
we've wandered to,
has always been fated.
And Gimli is but
a stop on the paths
of our wander.

Flin Flon Falls to the Bearmen

steadiness of hand
release the stone into
cascading grind.

and Dudley's red handled rock finds a heaviness that carries it
with balanced weight past the guards and into the house

balanced Mistahaya
gathers final stone
above the hack

looks to Northwind and with the slow motion of his hand
he pulls afternoon sun through the steady fall of snow.

sing song emerges
from webbing flesh
between fingers

and maskwanapewak raise and point their broom blades
to the building light as it erupts from the heavy clouds

nickel miners
buckled, rock balance
thrown off.

last of the yellow stones are hammered out by percussion gun
of Bearmen filled with the hunger of years of unanswered song.

Baptiste Pushes the Disciples Past the Spacemen

Rock grip warm
to touch, Lord's grace
courses through

to ice below lip of stone, phantom energy makes granite buoyant
guides it through & past hash marks, rests in second orbit house.

Lacroix sweeps
hard before stone cast,
to bend earth with

friction, morphing of ice by the hands and pressure of engineers,
produces no movement of rock, Jesus' stone's orbit holds, another.

Pablo follows
with closed-eye push
off, then release

and the second to last stone spins at 45 rpm like his father's
Caetano Veloso album, smooth, breeze through an empty street

Baptiste glides
right foot on ice sheet,
left pushing

and the final stone finds its home, behind a wall built of spaceman
folly. They stand in reverence of a miracle, Jesus behind them, in
shock.

Marten Appears atop Shavings Pile Behind Gimli Curling Club

Seen, like fire atop
spit, dirt infused shavings
from the ice inside,
Waabizheshi appears
orange like rising sun.

Quiet, inquisitive, bold
eyes akin to blackness
between the ancestors
along the Great White Way.

He comes to Mistahaya,
out back throwing a wiz
at a nearby stand of birch.
Both give off slight moves,

adjustments against wind,
against cold, against pale
light at the tail end of Gimli.
Waabizheshi rises up,

meets his gaze and blurts
out a series of loud chirps
and clicks that he is certain
says *get it together, baby.*

And he bolts off, against
shadows, and into the trees.
Behind him, two crushed
drones, a sliver of tartan skin.

Eddie Puskamoose Shares Smokes with Northwind

It is strange that trouble
arrives from the west, less
strange that it arrives with
money enough to feed
us all. Yet we stand here,
those Roughneck boys in
the rink, with their tar sand
muck, sprinkling bad
medicine on every part
of Gimli they touch.

Mrs. Puskamoose has had
dreams of wildlife on *Murder
She Wrote,* and she blames
their arrival on the oil men
hauling up claiming everything
theirs, the Sinclair uptown
claim their rabbit ears only
pick-up CTV and OMNI.

Watch them. They are mastodons
of the old stories, ones that have
found their way back atop the ice.

Jesus is Cast Out of Swiss Chalet

Post-match, it is all quarter
chicken dinners, and Jann
Arden's greatest hits, chain
budget celebrations. Miracles
made flesh by following dance
steps atop unfamiliar surfaces.
Jesus, Pablo, Baptiste, Juan,
seated beneath Bobby Hull
glamour shot, joyous in ways
that resemble nearly forgotten
family holidays. The action
they will say was quick,
like a goldeye school
glimmering at lake surface
before fleeing under
currents and waves.

Jesus, halted
as he walked past table
nearest bar, held by outstretched
roughneck arm. The question
asks if his buddy has
been putting moves
on the other rink's squaw.

The act came,
like lightning
from a blue sky,
struck their table
from below let out
a sound akin to
three derricks
collapsing
without
government subsidy,
and the tears of grown
men that follow their
toys are taken away.

Jesus may have
been restrained
by off-duty garbage
men, Pablo may
have been hit
with a gravy cup,
but Baptiste was certain,
Roughnecks
were not lords,
that they cowered
when furniture,
hot food, cutlery
are hurled at them.

Half-Light

And play was set up through a series of losses and poor ends and good ends that the Bearmen would face the Roughnecks for the bonspiel final. The astronauts noticed, back at the bar in the inn, that their cell phones dropped every call with the 450-area code. Outside the edges of Lake Winnipeg, where ice met rock, glowed with half-light. The empty sky punctuated by the passing flares of space debris muscling in against the atmosphere. That night the shortwave fizzed and failed. Lacroix left the static on and watched out his darkened window.

the medicine lines of the
curling rink
throbbed with the ancestors
dancing
on its surface

behind it: a stocky figure
moved in
small circles to cracks
between static.

Grandmother Rises Above the Gimli Memorial Curling Centre

Grandmother transforms
into Deep Snow Moon,
casts upon her children
a bath of translucent blue,
coats trees, rocks, sedans,
traffic lights in pale fire
reminder that night is simply
a day gone dormant. Light
pales but never fully extinguishes.

Leaned against door frame,
Northwind finds Nosemaskwa
glossed with the light of 400
years of murdered relations,
hunched over, she watches
grandmother cresting trees,
offers granola bar bite to Northwind.
Twin clouds of warm breath
pushing the cold away between

them. Deep-soul level tired
courses through both of them,
the longevity of fight handed
them fate weighs heavier than
those unaware of the motions
of all thirteen heaves, how that
motion drives their lives, dips
the world in its unending pale

council fire. Nosemaskwa says
to be sure, you've dreamed
of martens. Ravens haunt
mine, and they descend
to rest behind the mountains.
Once this is done, the need
is to answer all these visions.

Northwind knows that nothing
is accomplished alone, that
his path is tied to those who
have come before him as gifts
along his path. That the light
of ancestors is that which is
the undying light, that which
gives birth to visions, guides
upon the impossibility of making
one's way through the tangle of
Creation coupled with colonial rule.

Sunrise on Lake Winnipeg Greets Day Three

Grandfather ignites
day, wind-blown gossamer
lingers on shore rocks.

Roughneck Skip Speaks with Dudley

Light refractured along
trophy skin, provides no
reflection of the creature
before Dudley, rather
the hundred-fold mirror
of a rebuilt Marten,
lay blank before the men.
Its surface, frozen, unsettled.

Before Dudley, Roughneck
Skip two-steps every reason
this game isn't for "latins,"
"trolls," "dorks," or "chugs."
He claims everything before
them as theirs and theirs
alone. Dudley feels a town
press their gaze up him
and Marten reflects
a blankness of ice and snow.

With head nod towards
Waabizheshi-Anangoog,
states, *I am bringing*
my relations home.

Nosemaskwa Sings Red Bone into the Inter-Tribal Circle

What's the matter with you, you feel right?
Do you feel the sky move, 'cause you're fine.
Baby, we need you to guide us in this night.
What's the matter with you, you feel right?
Don't feel right? Hail, bring it down, straight
down cause with it all, it's a matter of time.
What's the matter with you, you feel right?
Baby find it, come on and find it, you so divine

Canadarm Can't Save Spacemen from Roughnecks

Cicada hum
from fluorescent light
chases gallery voices

in the moments after the Roughneck Skip spins free
from around right guard, nestles stone in house centre.

Ice measured
by each angle, trajectory,
becomes math

and every answer approaches absolute zero. Dudley knows
the improbable is akin to impossible, and that no single stone

pressed into hand,
released mid-glide, hovering
atop ice warmed

by friction of broom sweeps, bent low, slay clear the house
of the roughneck. Recalls training, recalls a Canadarm

ionosphere sweep
casting debris from orbit.
Handful of comets.

Post release, no flares, no change. It fails. Lacroix declares unmoved
stones have overwhelmed training, observation, firm hand of reason.

Bearman Attend the Sermon Upon the Ice

Broom spun
between two palms.
Ease of shared motion.

Jesus delivers the parable of the stoned prep cook,
tells of exquisite movements forged in divine haze.

Baptiste lines up
stone, releases as fates
were determined

through the motions of hands guiding blades through
mustard greens, let know that he was guided by nature.

Stone slips into
the full house, nudging
relations before rest.

Dudley proclaims the gospel to be true, that one awakes
through the gift of sensing another new day, and greens

are for tea.
Final tally that finds
Bearmen's favour.

Their match of little reckoning to James Bricket, it rich
in the way councils exchange wampum, merge stories.

Ancestors Descend to Earth Outside the Gimli Curling Complex

At the end of the third day,
they return. Flitter in pale
whisps above the town,
settled into a stern huddle
as a depth of coldness
descends upon it all. Await
what is to follow, stones
that must be cast, exits
that must still be made.

Bearmen Topple the Roughnecks with Flurry of Stones

Left guard
collapses, impact
spins rock out

of circle, exposing the Roughneck's lead stone. A centre held
solely by the stubbornness of granite being unwilling to move.

Slider foot
passes the hack,
stone set free.

The path, typically filled with cacophony of demands, of calls
to bend the earth itself, is lit by the building melody she begins.

Stone speeds
past Bearmen, a comet
returning home.

The song grows, spreads, and it's all na, na, la, na, na, la and
bells ringing as stone drives down upon final Roughneck rock.

Rocks meet
in solid body clunk,
crescendo of song.

Gallery erupts in chorus as the ice retreats before the roughneck
stance. Over collective voices they did not hear the earth itself break.

Eighth Vision at Gimli Brings Closure

At Lake Winnipeg shore line,
they appear
to Northwind,
emerging from birch stand,
in debate
over Waawaatesi
being able to calm
the Nain Rouge,
stop a city consuming fire.

Tecumseh insists
there is no fire in this vision,
simply the reminder
to follow a path.

They join Northwind seated
in Giant Tiger
camp chairs,
share chalky pastel Mentos
between them. Girty takes four.
We saw the Marten,
splayed out, at rest,
across the northern sky.
This bonspiel came
to its fateful completion.
We witnessed
highlights on TSN Eleven,
felt
ground shake
as Western Alienation
spun its oily body back to life.

And Lake Winnipeg is still enough
to be the ice at the Peter Glint,
and Tecumseh is pulling in
DeMaurier hauls,
unfiltered, and letting them fly
into clouds
above them all.

Crow watching.

One fights over land
as symbol,
Creator knows that nothing is
owned, simply gifted for a time,
and that mirror ball
of a marten
is as much a worthy symbol
as any patch of ice upon Creation.

Migrate like your relations.
Migrate like your ancestors.
All of Creation gifted
by your medicine step.

The Departure

In a world that knows larger battles
provide little but martyrs, the GMC
conversion van sputters to life before
the front steps of Northwind's single
wide. Mistahaya behind wheel,
revs the atavistic V8, shadow-
boxing the grunts of awakening
relations deep in the northern woods.
A call to rattle their hibernation,
let them know the thaw shall bring
forth what was long dormant,
that Waabizheshi-Anangoog shall
come home to God's Lake, reflect
the light of the ancestors a hundred
fold and shine through the darkest
days with a thousand embers
of what it is necessary to come.

They leave, in much the same
way they arrived. Windows up,
the frame of the van shaking
with the woodland honour beats
of a familiar AM rock song. Atop
his stoop Northwind witnesses
their migration, as the van pulls
down the drive way and vanishes
in the tree stands between here
and the highway north.

Dawn returns with the hustle of clouds
ushered across open spaces between stars
against the deep blue of ice on the move
and nearby and distant stirrings of trees.
And the Bearmen depart Gimli, one less
in number, with steadfast motion of nijii
positioned by stars, held firm by earth itself.

To Jasper, Northwind Departs

She pays for train tickets,
a pair,
with the better half
of 50/50 money.

Highway 9 south punctuated
by migrating geese,
commuting Nissans,
Hondas, half-tons.

Eddie at wheel,
Sven the advisor,
they speak volumes
of economic development
of full hotels, of it all

happening outside of the money season.

Nosemaskwa nods
to stories of Icelandic ancestors,
difficulty of fishing, impossibility
of tourists, cottagers.

Northwind speaks
of a pathway complete,
the keys to his single wide,
unlikelihood of returns.

Nosemaskwa states
We must be like terns,
Grandmother of the South's
warm touch, Grandfather of the West's
tempest of movements, our map
to Creation, our seasonal selves.

Golden Boy peers out
from atop bare branches
above Broadway, hand
extended northward.

Northwind knows
this is the last of his Gimli
visions, that the view north
shall be taken care of.

Westward to the ancestors
Westward to the mountaintops
to dance with them
shower in their medicine

Westward with the only woman
that is more home than Creation itself.

VIA Rail Train One departs westward
and snakes its path like a fledging river
placing, caressing each gift of earth, for
the first time since a long hibernation.

Nosemaskwa Sings Marshall Tucker Band into Our Closing Night

The ancestors they descend, can't you see
them sending us off. Gonna take a freight train,
down at the station, Lord, head off to a place
where mountain meets sky, can't you see
gonna climb me a mountain, gotta face
up those ancestors, greet them like a refrain
to a song we can't forget. Can't you see
the highest mountain? Godspeed this train.

Acknowledgments

The author would like to thank the Ontario Arts Council and the Canada Council for the Arts for the generous funding to undertake and complete this project. The very first drafts of this work were completed under the guidance of Maura Stanton at Indiana University. A profound debt of gratitude is owed to her and my fellow workshop members in helping to coax fire from early sparks for this book. An immense gratitude is also extended to the excellent literary journals and anthologies where the following poems first appeared and whose editors and publishers contributed to the production of these poems in their current form.

"Rise of the New Prophet" originally published as
"Legend of the Bearmen Rising" *Retirement Plan,* Issue 3 2019.

"From Sobey's Emerges the Short Order Rink"
Retirement Plan, Issue 5, 2020.

"This Fire Born of Distant Volcanoes"
Anti-Languorous Project No. 7, summer 2020.

"Crow Carries the Word to Three Oceans"
Anti-Languorous Project No. 7. summer 2020.

"Northwind Dreams She Makes Fire Dance"
Rialto, No.5, Spring 2021.

"Bearmen Greet Fresh Day, Hibernation Ends"
Rialto, No.5, Spring 2021.

"Chocolate Walnut Cruller Vision" *Rialto,* No.5, Spring 2021.

"Eddie Puskamoose Showers History at the Main Street ACE Hardware" *FreeFall,* Vol. 31, issue 1. Spring 2021.

About the Author

D.A. Lockhart is the author of *Devil in the Woods* (Brick Books, 2019) and *Breaking Right* (Porcupine's Quill, 2020). His work has garnered multiple Pushcart Prize nominations and has been generously supported by the Ontario Arts Council and the Canada Council for the Arts. He is the publisher at Urban Farmhouse Press and poetry editor at the *Windsor Review.* A turtle clan citizen of the Moravian of the Thames First Nation, he currently resides at Waawiiyaatanong and Pelee Island.